For my husband, John Conheeney, and his four youngest grandchildren,
Thomas and Liam Tarleton and John and Oliver Conheeney
With love
—M. H. C.

In memory of George R. Kaiser Jr.—artist, teacher, and sailor
—W. M.

⌐ ACKNOWLEDGMENTS ⌐

Last year at a holiday signing, I was chatting with my longtime friend Wendell Minor, who illustrated four of my hardcover novels, including my first book, *Where Are the Children?*

His editors, Rubin Pfeffer and Paula Wiseman, were there and suggested Wendell and I collaborate on a children's book. *Ghost Ship* is the result of that conversation. Cheers and blessings to you, Rubin and Paula, for after making the suggestion, guiding us in the process of writing and illustrating this story.

Elizabeth Reynard's *The Narrow Land: Folk Chronicles of Old Cape Cod* and *The Mooncussers of Cape Cod*, by Henry C. Kittredge, gave me a great sense of life in the seventeenth century on my beloved Cape Cod.

I have so enjoyed going back in time to tell this tale and having Wendell Minor's exquisite illustrations to bring it to life.

—M. H. C.

A special thanks to Mary Higgins Clark for sharing her love and lore of Cape Cod, and to Rubin Pfeffer and Paula Wiseman for making this collaboration a joyous experience.

The illustrator also wishes to thank David Murdoch, of Chatham Water Tours, and the Chatham Historical Society for an in-depth perspective on the history and waters of Chatham, Massachusetts, and marine artist Mark Myers, whose illustrations in John Harland's *Seamanship in the Age of Sail* (Naval Institute Press, 1984) were extremely helpful.

Although *Ghost Ship* is a work of fiction, the illustrator has made every effort to infuse the paintings in this book with a sense of time and place.

—W. M.

SIMON & SCHUSTER BOOKS FOR YOUNG READERS · An imprint of Simon & Schuster Children's Publishing Division · 1230 Avenue of the Americas, New York, New York 10020 · Text copyright © 2007 by Mary Higgins Clark · Illustrations copyright © 2007 by Wendell Minor · All rights reserved, including the right of reproduction in whole or in part in any form. · SIMON & SCHUSTER BOOKS FOR YOUNG READERS is a trademark of Simon & Schuster, Inc. · Book design by Wendell Minor · The text for this book is set in Edwardian Medium. · The illustrations for this book are rendered with gouache watercolor on Strathmore bristol paper. · Manufactured in the United States of America · 1 2 3 4 5 6 7 8 9 10 · Library of Congress Cataloging-in-Publication Data · Clark, Mary Higgins. · Ghost ship / Mary Higgins Clark ; illustrated by Wendell Minor. — 1st ed. · p. cm. · "A Paula Wiseman book." · Summary: While visiting his grandmother on Cape Cod, nine-year-old Thomas encounters a ship's cabin boy from centuries past. · ISBN-13: 978-1-4169-3514-8 · ISBN-10: 1-4169-3514-2 · [1. Cape Cod (Mass.)—Fiction. 2. Seafaring life—Fiction.] I. Minor, Wendell, ill. II. Title. · PZ7.C5493Gh 2007 · [E]—dc22 · 2006032338

first edition

Ghost Ship
A CAPE COD STORY

MARY HIGGINS CLARK

Ghost Ship

A CAPE COD STORY

Illustrated by WENDELL MINOR

A PAULA WISEMAN BOOK · SIMON & SCHUSTER BOOKS FOR YOUNG READERS

NEW YORK · LONDON · TORONTO · SYDNEY

Summer had begun and Thomas was visiting his grandmother who lived in a very old house in Cape Cod that had once belonged to a sea captain. Sometimes she told him stories about the great sailing ships that had come to Cape Cod many years ago from all over the world. She told him that in the old days when a storm suddenly began, a ship trying to reach harbor would be driven into the rocks and sand bars, where it would break up and sink.

Thomas loved to hear the stories. He wondered about the sea captain who had built this house more than two hundred years ago. He wondered if that sea captain ever lost a ship in a storm. He thought about that a lot.

One day Thomas went down the long flight of stairs from the lawn to the beach. He had promised his grandmother that he would not go too near the water until she joined him. His grandmother knew that Thomas would never break his word.

There had been a heavy storm the night before. The wind had whipped the waves until they slammed halfway up the stairs before crashing back onto the shore. Now the beach was littered with shells and rocks that had been washed in by the sea. Thomas began to sift sand through his fingers. The sand was damp, but he liked that.

Sometimes after a storm he would find unusual things that had been in the ocean. Once he had even found a small ring. His grandmother said it wasn't valuable but that it looked as though it had been in the ocean for a long, long time.

He wondered if after the big storm last night it was possible that he would find another ring. Or maybe he'd come upon an unbroken shell. If he did find one, he would put it up to his ear and listen, because shells hold the sound of the sea.

But then, suddenly, his fingers felt a hard metal object. He had to dig around it to set it free. It was much heavier than a shell. It looked very, very old. He ran his fingers over it and began to rub the sand and salt from it. But it was like trying to rub cement off a wall. He looked around and reached for a big rock and began to try to scrape the crust off whatever it was he was holding in his hand.

seen bl
second
1752, I
crashed

knew I was strong and could be of great use passing buckets of water. But it was not to be."

Thomas was no longer aware of how chilly it had become. He wanted to hear the rest of the story.

"I had gone but a short distance when I heard the sound of a horse approaching. I stepped aside and observed that it was none other than Samuel Lewis, a sorry excuse for a man. I knew what he was up to. He had given the appearance of joining the firefighters and then when they rushed out of the village, had held his horse back, confident that in the confusion he would not be missed."

"He sounds like a coward," Thomas said.

"A coward he was and far worse than that. When he was captain of his own ship, he was a most careless mariner, and when a storm came up, his sails were shredded and his ship wallowed in the sand. Twenty-six brave sailors were drowned because of him.